Harry's Lovely Spring Day

n.g.k.

Illustrated by Janelle Dimmett

ngk - To Janelle - Couldn't have done this without you.

First published in the UK and USA on 27th January 2018. This version published in April 2018.
A huge thank you to Sylva Fae for everything. The advice, writing help, and support.
Thanks to Wendy Hobbs for everything you've done. Thanks to HH and KH for checking things through.
Thanks to Millie for editing help!

2nd Edition

Katie and
Harry's Bridge

The Sugar Mill

Katie's Cake Shop

Book 1:

Spring

On the crest of a wave and the wisp of the wind,

Harry the Happy Mouse was thinking good things.

He lived in the city all on his own.

With a stone for a chair and a box for a home.

Harry was happy, but then one day....

...the wind was wild and his box blew away!

The day turned to night and it started to thunder!

"I'm soaking!" said Harry.

"I'll find something to hide under."

Just then a stranger walked down the street,
  "Wow!" said Harry, "I have someone to meet!"

"Excuse me," said the stranger, "Are you ok?
  It makes me so sad to see you this way!"

"I'm fine," said Harry, "Just a spot of bad luck,
  this weather is better for a fish or a duck!"

"My name is Katie," said the mouse with a smile.
The stranger stopped to talk for a while.

"Take these things!" said Katie,
"You need them more than me,
I'm just about to leave for the country you see."

"Wow!" said Harry, "Are you sure?
   I really don't think I need them more."

"It's fine," said Katie, "It'll make me feel grand!
   It's always nice to lend someone a hand!"

"Thank you!" said Harry, "I don't know what to say!
   This has turned out to be a really good day!"

Katie shouted "Goodbye Mr. Mouse! It's really no fuss!"
As she sat on the back of a country bound bus.

Harry snuggled down to a dry quiet night,
He woke the next day to the sun shining bright.

Harry left for the country that sunny spring day.
"I have to thank Katie, I must find a way!

It might be quite far, it might take some time,
With rivers to cross and hills to climb!"

He jumped on a train,

a car,

and a bike.

A balloon and a van,

a bus and a trike!

Harry had travelled so far from the city,
The country was wild, so bright and so pretty.

"Now to find Katie!" said Harry with a grin.
While butterflies and ladybirds danced around him.

Harry walked along and found a Cow selling flour.
    "I really didn't think I'd see anyone at this hour!"

"Excuse me Mrs. Cow, could you help me?
    I'm looking for someone, where could she be?"

"Of course!" said the Cow, "Now let me see.
    Who are you looking for, who could she be?"

"Thank you!" said Harry, "Her name is Katie.
    She's small, she's brown and a mouse like me!"

"I have met Katie!" said the Cow with a smile.
    "Though I have to admit, it's been quite a while."

"She buys lots of flour, I don't know the reason.
    She's not here too often, perhaps once a season."

"Thank you!" said Harry, "That's a really good clue!
    I'll keep on looking, it was nice to meet you!"

"

Harry walked along and found a Cat.
  "Hello!" said Harry, "Could we have a quick chat?

Sorry to bother you, but could you help me?
  I'm looking for someone, where could she be?"

"Of course," said the Cat, "Now let me see.
    Who are you looking for, who could she be?"

"Thank you!" said Harry, "Her name is Katie,
    She's small, she's brown and a mouse like me!"

"I have met Katie!" said the Cat with a smile.
    "Though I have to admit, it's been quite a while."

"She buys lots of sugar, I don't know the reason.
    She's not here too often, perhaps once a season."

"I've got it!" said Harry, "After everything you've said!
    She needs sugar and flour to make cakes and bread!"

"I've found you, I've found you!" shouted Harry with glee!
   "I really hope that you're happy to see me?"

"I am!" said Katie with the happiest cheer.
   "I really hoped that you would find your way here."

Harry was happy and ever so glad!
   He went on to tell Katie of the journey he'd had.

"When you helped me that night it made me feel grand,
   Isn't it great to lend someone a hand?"

"Don't worry!" said Katie, "It was something so small.
   You really don't have to thank me at all!"

"I do." said Harry, "That's it you see,
   It was small for you but big for me!"

"When you do something small you can change someone's day,
Do something nice or have something to say!"

Minutes turned to hours and hours turned to days,

Days turned to weeks, in a beautiful spring haze.

"You know," said Harry, "You've changed my life,
Would you like to be my wife?"

"Of course!" said Katie, "Let's stay here forever!
I'll always be happy as long as we're together."

Harry and Katie were married soon after,
With flowers, balloons and plenty of laughter.

"Wow!" said Harry, "I just have to say,
    Thank you for making my lovely spring day!"

"When you helped me that night, it made me feel grand,
    I will always try to lend someone a hand."

On the crest of a wave and the wisp of the wind,

Harry the Happy Mouse was thinking good things.

Other books in the bestselling Harry The Happy Mouse Series:

Book 1 — Harry's Lovely Spring Day

Book 2 — Harry The Happy Mouse

Book 3 — Harry's Spooky Surprise

Book 4 — Harry The Christmas Mouse

Please visit:
www.harrythehappymouse.com

CPSIA information can be obtained
at www.ICGtesting.com
Printed in the USA
LVHW071415110520
655361LV00025B/2769